Poems by Marilyn Singer

The Morgans Dream

Illustrations by Gary Drake

Henry Holt and Company

New York

All the Morgans

Suppertime they fill
   the room to bursting
all the Morgans
     Dad serving
       Mom settling
     Daisy the dog scrounging for food
   Grandma and Grandpa, too,
      paying a visit
     to count Sara's jokes
       Amy's freckles
       Timothy's half-eaten cookies
       the baby's brand-new toes
Everyone together
   in the same world
After dinner they spill
   into the dappled yard
all the Morgans
      Mom singing
       Dad dancing
     Dooley the cat swatting at June bugs
   Grandma and Grandpa, too,
      staying the evening
     to watch Michael frown
       Catherine argue
       Mary read quietly in a corner
  till the shadows get too deep
   and the fireflies appear
   Then one by one
all the Morgans
   Grandma and Grandpa, too,
say good night and grow still
     to drift or run
      to swim or fly
to Dreamland
   sometimes together
   always alone
leaving the same world far behind

Catherine's Dream

The words
　　all mumbly jumbly
are not her own
No matter how hard she tries
　　she talks in
　　　　　　twisted biscuits
　　　and fumphfarumphfary
Jimmy, Johnny
　　Patsy, Pauline
　　　　the whole class
　　　　　whinny and wicker
　　like tickled horses
The underwear
　　all purple and yellow
is not her own
She can't imagine why
　　she's wearing it
　　　　　　with orange galoshes
　　and fluffy wuffy furbelows
Lizzie, Linda
　　Brian, Bob
　　　　the whole class
　　　　　hoot and halloo
　　like crazy chimpanzees
The dream
　　all dummy crummy
is not her own
Though she wouldn't believe it
　　if you told her
　　　　　　dreamers everywhere squirm
　　in the same tongue-tied misery
　　　before a howdy rowdy crowd
Except their underwear is always
　　different

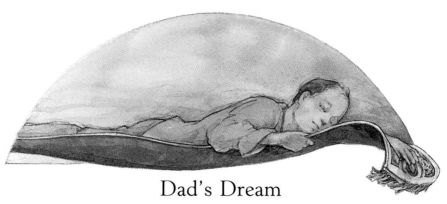

Dad's Dream

He likes to say he has American days
    and Arabian nights
In this evening's dream
    like a prince on a magic carpet
Dad and his desk fly right out his office window
    (leaving his boss in the middle of a word)
        into the eye blue sky
High he goes and higher
    till the soaring buildings shrink
        to pencils stuck in a cup
    and wide rushing rivers narrow
        to trickling ink
Soon the whole city is gone
    torn away like the top page of a memo pad
Below becomes country green
Dad and his desk drift down to a mazy field
    and skim the secret paths
        shielded by cornstalks
until he finds clustered there in the very heart
    his family
        saluting him with horns and drums
See you later, he assures them
Then he waves and glides right on

Sara's Dream

She's alone
    and she isn't
On a beach
    but it isn't
And before she has time
    to think
        Do I want to
          take a swim
She dives down
          down
             down
    under a strange sea
Whales waltz by
    with diamond wings
Ruby lobsters ramble
        Pearly jellyfish parachute
Silver-legged octopi loop the loop
She's a mermaid
    and she isn't
She is dreaming
    but she isn't
And before she can say
    let me stay here forever
She floats up
       up
     up
    to her dark dry bed
      missing the magic
        she left behind

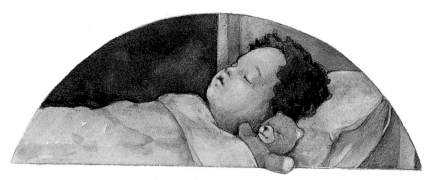

Amy's Dream

One time it was yellow
    with eyes like stoplights
        and teeth like spikes
Another time it wore armor
        its face hidden in a rusty mask
        its feet clomp clank clodding
            step by step
            by step by step
Once it was spider's leg hairy
        Once it was scorpion smooth
Tonight it crawls cold and green
        a cross between a crocodile
            and a cobra
Hissing and gurgling
        rissing and churgling
it slowly slowlies into her room
But Amy's even slower
        stuck to her bed
            like britches on brambles
It attacks
        She shrieks
She smacks
        It speaks
            changing right before her eyes
                into Sara complaining
                    "You woke me from a good dream"
Then sleepily they switch beds
        so Sara can fight off any nightmare
            that dares to climb inside

Daisy's Dream

Air running in the dark
    Daisy the dog dreams
        of the park
            she visits every day
With muffled snuffling
    she greets
        the beagle from the bike shop
        the dachshund from next door
        two palsy-walsy poodles
        three spaniels
        five mutts
With quiet chomping
    she eats
        forbidden chicken bones
        moldy rolls
        stale pretzels
        fresh grass
    (she lets the squishy peaches pass)
With muted woofing
    she meets
        flying Frisbees
        fleeing squirrels
        almost homers
        kids to kiss
For Daisy awake
    or Daisy dreaming
        a visit to the park is
            bliss

Mary's Dream

There's a wrongness in her dream
    like a picture hanging backward
    like a puppet dangling upside down
She can feel it on her shoulders
    like a pack she used to carry
    like a pair of missing wings
Something gone
    that ought to be there
Something empty
    that should be full
Drifting from room to room
    in the silent vacant house
she searches the shifting shadows
She would right it if she knew
    what was crooked
She could find it if she knew
    what was lost

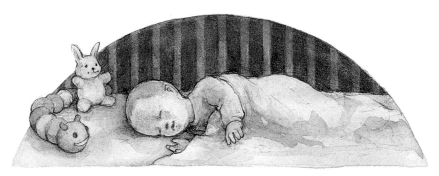

Kevin's Dream

Baby's a beginner
     even at dreaming
  shaping familiar pictures
    while he sleeps—
a fondle of flannel
    a keep safe of crib
a quiet of crooning
    a wailing of thirst
a shaft of sunlight shocking
    a ring of arms rocking
            rocking

Mom's Dream

Noise
     a whole lot of noise
a caterwauling screaking squalling
     thunderation of noise
Like timpanis fighting
     with out-of-tune cellos
or donkeys bawling out
     boisterous geese
How can a dream be so loud, she puzzles
     rapping once twice on the breakfast table
Just like that
     the hubbub stops
     the kitchen becomes a concert hall
     and her children—
          Mary, Michael, Timothy
          Catherine, Sara, Amy—
     standing in a circle on the softly lit stage
          sing
"Marmalade. Please pass the marmalade"
          in perfect harmony
while she waves her baton and marvels
     at the baby singing bass

Dooley's Dream

Just a push push away
    milk sweet and tasty
Just a nudge nudge nearby
    mother warm and cushy
On the rug he lies dreaming
    of kitten time comforts
        while opening, closing grown-up cat paws

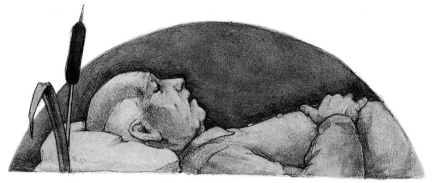

Grandpa's Dream

In the lake
    ("Pond," says Michael)
Grandpa swims
    with the red dog and the yellow dog
        one pushing through the pickerelweed
        the other snapping at sticks
          Both long gone
    ("Dead," declares Michael)
Grandpa knows this is so
But as he pats the wet shaggy backs
        sees the cold noses snorting
           thick paws paddling
           lop ears twitching away pesky flies
He knows too that things can come back to life
    in dreams
He will share this secret some day
    with Michael, he thinks
Then he opens his mouth and laughs
    silent and merry
      like the red dog and the yellow dog
        churning happily
    through the calm green water

Michael's Dream

Everywhere he looks there are babies
    big fat melon-bellied babies
    small pink babbling babies
        winky babies
        stinky babies
in the bathtub
    in the basement
in the kitchen
    in his room
Here comes another one
    somebody (maybe Grandpa) yells
And Michael already dreaming
    sees himself on a desert island
where everywhere he looks there are monkeys
    plump monkeys round and shaggy as coconuts
    long skinny monkeys with pipe-cleaner tails
        grumpy monkeys
        jumpy monkeys
in the palm trees
    on the boulders
on his shoulders
    in his hair
Here comes another one
    somebody (maybe Grandpa) hollers
And Michael no longer dreaming
    tiptoes out into the garden
to spend some moments alone
    with the one and only moon

Timothy's Dream

Beware the such-a-much
     his mother told him
He never thought she meant
     in a dream
But there it is
     right before his goggling eyes
        steaming fizzling
        gleaming sizzling
     an explosion
       an eruption
         a such-a-much of food
Bagels bologna burritos
    Tutti-frutti strudel
Oozy éclairs
    Woozy cupcakes
Double chocolate
    Triple chocolate
Quadruple zip your lips with chocolate
Should he eat an eggroll
      wolf a waffle
       gobble a great bowl of guacamole
        or a pile of pastrami
         with pickles on the side?
No matter how his belly bur-bur-burbles
      his mouth waters
      his mind stews
No matter how he ogles
        boggles
He simply cannot choose

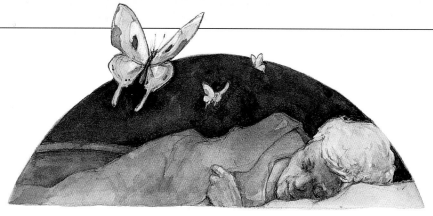

Grandma's Dream

In a sunlit room
    Grandma holds a necklace
"Precious gold," she murmurs
    stringing a seventh bright bead
"Precious gold," she whispers
    as it plinks into place
She feels the sunlight
    on her face
      and smiles
Six times before she has had this dream
Like a friend it comes
    warmer with each visit
Now it seems to her everything is
    shining
Room
    necklace
      heart
        world
"Precious gold," she tells the luminous air
    "Precious, precious gold."

Morning

Morning, the wrens trill
          And one by one
all the Morgans
          Grandma and Grandpa, too,
                drift or skim
                     swim or fly
from Dreamland
          to breakfast
Everyone in the same world
          sometimes alone
               and always
                    in some way
together

To Taro, my "other sister"
— M. S.

To Beverly and Harley
— G. D.

Acknowledgments
Thanks to Steve Aronson, Simone Kaplan, and everyone else at Holt.
Special thanks to Sara Livingston for her whales with
diamond wings, and to her sister, Amy.
— M . S .

Henry Holt and Company, Inc./*Publishers since 1866*
115 West 18th Street/New York, New York 10011
Henry Holt is a registered
trademark of Henry Holt and Company, Inc.
Text copyright © 1995 by Marilyn Singer
Illustrations copyright © 1995 by Gary Drake
All rights reserved.
Published in Canada by Fitzhenry & Whiteside Ltd.,
195 Allstate Parkway, Markham, Ontario L3R 4T8.
Library of Congress Cataloging-in-Publication Data
Singer, Marilyn.
The Morgans dream / poems by Marilyn Singer;
illustrations by Gary Drake.
Summary: A collection of poems relating the nighttime
dreams of a large family.
1. Dreams—Juvenile poetry.   2. Family—Juvenile poetry.
3. Children's poetry, American.   [1. Dreams—Poetry.   2. Family
life—Poetry. 3. American poetry.] I. Drake, Gary, ill. II. Title.
PS3569.I546M67 1995 811'.54—dc20   95-1718
ISBN 0-8050-3004-2
First Edition—1995
The artist used Nu-Pastels pastels on Rives heavyweight
paper to create the illustrations for this book. The spot art was
created using Pelikan watercolors on T.H. Saunders paper.
Printed in the United States of America
on acid-free paper.∞
1 3 5 7 9 10 8 6 4 2